INTEGRATE

Chrissie Parker

Dear Corrina,

Thank you for all of your support over the years! :)

ChrissiePxx

First published in 2013

ISBN-13: 978-1493737338
ISBN-10: 1493737333

Dedication

"It never rains in Southern California"
Anthony Read Ellwood
16 October 1936 – 26 December 2011

ONE

A full moon had risen high in the sky casting a brilliant silver glow over the dark world below. The night was, for the most part, silent and still, only occasionally disturbed by a cry of fox, hoot of owl or rustle of a small mammal in the hedgerow. A long, winding road lined with trees, hedges and fences, snaked its way through the vast open countryside. Now and again a lone building reared its head, the only sign of human habitation in an otherwise bleak landscape.

A solitary car wound its way along the inky tarmac, travelling at speeds faster than legally allowed, the headlights illuminating everything, casting an eerie glow on the road ahead. Despite the low temperature, the roof was down and the driver had one hand on the steering wheel as the other dangled carelessly over the top of the door. A lit cigarette glowed orange in his free fingers and ash floated away in the night air, falling like light grey snow to the receding tarmac.

Jack glanced up at the moon. It was so clear and bright that he could see a multitude of grey craters dotted across the surface of the natural satellite. It was strange to be driving in the middle of the night with nothing but the darkness, moon and stars for company, but it matched his sombre mood and brought him comfort.

This time of year was never good; morbidity fell upon Jack like a blanket, smothering him, leaving him restless, uncomfortable and barely able to breathe. He had hoped it would get easier as the years passed but the guilt and depression remained and threatened to completely envelop him, sending him hurtling into the abyss. However hard he tried, he just couldn't shake it.

Jack's piercing dark eyes stayed on the route ahead, as he steered the vehicle through every curve and switchback the road threw at him. On the straights, he pushed the accelerator further to the floor, teasing the car, forcing it to go faster, the speed thrilling him. He glanced in the rear-view mirror and caught sight of his own reflection. Sometimes he barely recognised himself. His messy jet black hair, tossed around by the breeze, was in serious need of a wash and cut; it hung unevenly about his face, at times falling into his eyes, momentarily blocking his view. His demeanour and looks gave him a handsome yet wolf-like quality and people never quite knew what to make of him, making them reluctant to seek him out. Not that he cared; he preferred his own company anyway.

Jack had no idea where he was heading. All he knew was that he just had to get in the car and drive until it was out of his system, however long that may take. Lifting the cigarette to his lips, he inhaled deeply; with each breath the soothing nicotine calmed him. Slowly exhaling, he released the blue-grey smoke to the elements before finally throwing the spent butt to the road. As it hit the ground, it sparked a brilliant orange, the only vibrancy of colour in the dark night.

The car, an accelerating spectacle of chrome, engine and throttle, continued on its journey to nowhere eating up miles of shimmering blacktop which steadily disappeared into the dark night.

*

A burning fire in a wrought iron grate flickered bright hues of yellow and orange, crackling and spitting as the flames greedily ate their way through the logs. The old brick fireplace surrounding it had been built into the side of the room upon construction of the house and was topped with an old oak mantelpiece. Photo frames, trinkets and burning candles were haphazardly strewn across the oak surface, the focal point of an otherwise plain and gloomy room. No pictures hung on the walls, there was little furniture and not even the floor had been carpeted. The bare boards had been sanded and treated but still creaked and groaned with every movement of the old house.

An unlit electric bulb, seldom used, hung overhead collecting dust and drapes were drawn across large sash windows so that the only light in the room came from the candles and fireplace. At the centre of the room was a solitary wooden table. On its surface lay a small wooden box, with brass hinges and an intricately carved lid. A strikingly beautiful woman was seated in a wooden chair next to the table. Her long, thick blonde hair tumbled over her shoulders, the ends brushing the table. Her skin was porcelain pale, which only enhanced the deep cerulean blue of her eyes. Her long slender arms were adorned with a collection of bangles that tinkled and rattled as she moved her delicate limbs. Reaching forward, she opened the lid of the box and removed its contents, a pack of tarot cards wrapped in a square of red silk.

Revealing the cards she placed the red silk on the table, smoothing it flat, and moved the box to one side. Clasping the cards in her hands Corinne closed her eyes and breathed deeply, focusing her mind, clearing it of clutter. The cards remained steady in her delicate hands, patiently waiting for her to make the next move. Stillness enveloped the room; the only disturbance was the flicker of a single candle, as she allowed herself to commune with the cards.

*

Jack steered the car along the seemingly endless road. Turning on the radio he was greeted by dulcet tones of aging, faded rock stars; loud noisy sounds that pierced the silence before bleeding themselves into the passing night. Lighting another cigarette, he inhaled deeply before throwing his lighter onto the passenger seat. Bored of the current song, he reached for the radio, flicking through the channels until he landed on a station that by some fluke of luck was playing his favourite tune. It was like listening to an old familiar friend, and he tapped his fingers in time on the steering wheel, his mood lightening in an instant.

It wasn't long before the DJ changed tracks,

and Jack's mood changed again, spiralling, dragging him back into the pit of despair he often languished in. He wanted that high again, needed it. Reaching to the passenger seat once more he lifted a bottle of bourbon. Placing it between his legs he unwrapped it, unscrewed the lid and lifted the bottle to his lips, swallowing the sweet nectar, enjoying the taste as it burnt its way down to his stomach. Placing the bottle back between his knees, he took another drag on his cigarette, and exhaled smoke into the night.

Jack was numb. The feeling was not unusual, but it was much worse than it had ever been before. He just couldn't shake the despondency that had gripped him of late. It was as though he were on a precipice, with dark storm clouds gathering and billowing around him. Impending doom and gloom making him feel as though the only option he had was to fall and submit himself to the never-ending darkness. People told him it was understandable. They also said he would start to feel better, and that the pain would eventually pass. He was still waiting for that day, but as yet it hadn't arrived. With each new waking day, it fell further and further from his grasp, and he had no choice but to succumb to the constant torture of his heart-laden grief.

*

Corinne's eyes fluttered open. She was still shuffling the tarot cards, concentrating on them, and them alone. Once content, she placed the deck face down in the centre of the table and closed her eyes once more. Only when her mind was completely clear did she ask the question, silently.

Finally, she opened her eyes and cut the deck with her left hand before allowing the cards to speak to her. She chose seven cards from the deck at random, placing them face down on the silk cloth in the shape of a horseshoe. Returning the excess cards to the wooden box, she breathed deeply, retaining her concentration before turning the first card.

The Empress.

It hit her like a bolt of lightning, sending waves of nausea and dizziness through her, leaving her skin trembling and tingling. For a split second everything went dark, candles flickered and sputtered, trying their best to fight the unknown forces and stay lit. The drapes parted, flapping with a sudden movement of air and she felt a gust of breeze on her face. The moon's gentle light sought the crack in the drapes and bathed itself across her skin and the fire dimmed to all but faint embers.

She saw a long winding road, a car and fleeting glimpses of the town, like favourite memories played out on an old film projector. In silence she allowed the vision to reveal itself to her. The old school where she had laughed, played and learned appeared before her. The fields where she had lain in the sun, the river where she had splashed looking for fish, with a battered old net that had belonged to her father. The Church, a place so fixed in her memory that it was as much a part of her history as her own genes, and finally the house where she had grown up, and now sat.

As quickly as it had happened, everything returned to normal and she was back in the still, silent room. Corinne's heart plummeted, and she felt fear creep up her spine making her nerves jangle. Her hands shook and she could barely focus.

Helena.

Helena was in grave danger.

TWO

The night was dry, bright and serene, if a little chilly. Helena liked nights like this. It made her feel as though she were the only person alive, as though she had the entire world to herself, and could go anywhere and do anything she wanted. She walked along a quiet street that was intermittently lit by the large old fashioned lamp posts she loved; part of what made this area of town so beautifully quaint. It had an old preserved quality with reminders of its history on every corner, features that had been protected so well by town authorities. It was the perfect place to grow up and live, and the people who lived there mirrored the town and its very essence. Tourists loved it too. It was a favourite place on the map for them to stop and spend time. They frequented the riverside restaurants, the quaint historic back streets and the vibrant bars. They absorbed the atmosphere, shopped and relaxed, all reluctant to finally leave, wishing they lived in the welcoming community, vowing to return again another time.

Sharp pain in her feet disturbed Helena from her reverie. They hurt from wearing heels that were too high, and trying to walk home in them really hadn't helped. If Corinne could see her now, she'd laugh and shake her head with exasperation. Corrine had always been the more sensible of the twins, much more like an older sister. Helena had been the mischievous and outgoing one, always adventurous and up for something new, never settling for the day-to-day grind. It was the only way their parents had been able to tell the difference between them; in looks they were identical in every way.

It had been a fun evening out with friends. Helena loved the vibrancy of the bars and restaurants in town. There were so many lovely places to sit, talk and eat, or dance until the early hours. Her one regret was that she hadn't been able to persuade Corinne to come with her. She worried so much about her sister, who chose to spend most of her time shut up in her house, locked away from the world. Try as she might,

Helena rarely persuaded Corinne to leave her safe haven, and it became increasingly worrisome. Corinne wasn't the only one to hurt when their parents died, but whereas Helena chose to live life to the full, Corinne had spiralled into loneliness and depression, stripping their parents' house of all but their most sentimental possessions. Hiding away within the four walls with only her memories and tarot for company, Corinne kept to herself carrying with her a loss that had become increasingly hard to bear.

Passing the small church where the twins had spent Sunday mornings with their parents, Helena smiled. It brought back so many wonderful memories. As churches went, it was small and unremarkable, but inside it had a hidden architectural beauty. She imagined it standing there for hundreds of years as the town's history weaved itself through the very fabric of its structure. How many people had stepped through its doors, how many had been baptised there, married there, buried there? She had wanted her life to become an integral part of it too, which was why she had married Jimmy there. Their wedding day had been bright and sunny, and she had freely given her heart, body and soul to the man she'd always loved, who had been at her side since school, and who she knew would be there for her for the rest of her life. It had been a beautiful day and they had been surrounded by her family, whom she loved and cared for just as much. It had been perfect.

Now it saddened her to think that Corinne had turned her back on it after the death of their parents, choosing instead to turn to a different kind of spiritual help, the kind that saw her surrounding her life with crystals, tarot and the occult. It was not a decision Helena agreed with, but Corinne was her sister and she loved her no matter what.

Stopping outside the house of God, she bent down to adjust the strap on her shoes in an effort to relieve the ache that was now affecting her calves. Her feet really were in agony now. Laughing quietly to herself, Helena could hear Corinne's disapproving voice in her head, telling her she should wear something more sensible next time.

As usual she knew Corinne was right.

*

Corinne breathed deeply, playing with the silver locket that hung about her neck. She could feel the strength of connection to Helena through it. It pulled at her, forcing a jumble of endless emotions to the surface. Why did she always feel this way, as though she had to constantly worry about and protect her sister?

Releasing the locket, Corinne brought her attention back to the cards. Candles flickered as wax slid down tapered columns, pooling on surfaces and in holders. Flames cast eerie shadows around the room giving it a homely, yet slightly haunting glow. The fire in the grate burned steadily, crackling and spitting as more logs surrendered themselves to the inevitable. Her hands still shook, but she had to continue. She couldn't stop now. Taking a deep breath she turned the next card.

The Emperor.

Fleetingly a long dark road appeared in her mind, a full moon shining overhead, but before she had the chance to examine it, it was gone. She tried to make sense of where the cards were taking her, and what they were trying to say. An uneasy feeling had settled in her stomach and she feared the worst. She knew Helena was involved somehow, but no more than that.

Who or what was the Emperor?

Maybe the Emperor was Jimmy, but she didn't feel that was the case. It was more likely the Emperor was an unknown person or force yet to come. If that were so, then it was almost certain that Helena *was* in danger. Only time would tell, and Corinne was already dreading the wait.

*

Grey laced clouds began to form and move across the dark sky as Jack continued his journey. The moon continued to bathe the surrounding countryside with ethereal silver light, and the silence remained. He lit another cigarette, allowing the thick smoke to envelop him. Tobacco was one of his favourite scents, and he savoured each blissful cigarette he smoked. The alcohol had started to numb him and it no longer burned when he took a swig. He could feel it flowing through his body, warming his blood and dulling his senses. Taking away the pain. He relaxed a little, enjoying the three things he loved most in the world: driving, smoking and drinking.

Glancing in the rear-view mirror, he caught his own reflection again. His bloodshot eyes were surrounded by dark circles; his face giving away his lack of sleep and fond affection for alcohol. He ran his hand through his dark mid-length hair, which was getting in his eyes again. It really did need a cut, another thing to add to the list of things he should do, but would probably forget to.

He was lost in life; had no direction.

Everything had been taken from him.

Getting up each day seemed to serve no purpose at all. Waking each morning to usher in a new day only reminded him of all that was missing from his life. The only peace he found was whilst asleep or staring into the bottom of a glass. If he were an animal, someone would have put him out of his misery. His life was like the road he was currently travelling: long, winding, dark and so very, very lonely.

THREE

Corinne sipped water from a tall glass that sat on the table next to her. Apprehension gripped her, making her hesitant. The tarot spread was like a bad omen weighing heavily upon her, summoning fear and dread and making her reluctant to turn the next card. She should stop now, reshuffle the cards and return them to the box, but she had never given up on a reading, and she wouldn't do so now. She had to be strong and see it through.

With shaky fingers, she cautiously turned the third card.

The Chariot.

Tightness gripped her throat and she could barely breathe. Her head swam and she felt the dizziness wash over her again, a faint noise of guttural car engine surrounded her, but she resisted the blackness, clawing her way back to the surface, even though the candles had already begun to flicker. Urgently without hesitation she turned the fourth card.

Death.

Corinne rose unsteadily to her feet, knocking over the chair in her desperation to distance herself from the spread. Standing with her back to the wall she closed her eyes, her breath deep and rasping, her hands shook and sweat had beaded on her brow. She tried to rid herself of the visions and nausea that was threatening to completely overwhelm her. She was a veteran at tarot reading and knew that she shouldn't take the cards at their literal meaning. Death didn't always mean *Death*, sometimes it just symbolised a change. But it wasn't just the spread. Her gut instinct was telling her that something was very wrong. The visions had seemed all too real and her intuition had never let her down before. Moving to the fireplace, she brushed her hand over the silver photo frame that sat on the mantelpiece containing a picture of her and Helena. Her sister meant the world to her, and she couldn't work out why she feared for her so much. Corinne had never experienced this before and it scared the hell out of her.

It had to be the twin connection; it had always been strong between them.

She could try and phone Helena but Corinne knew that she was useless at keeping her phone charged; sometimes she didn't even bother taking it with her. Corinne just didn't know what to do next. She was too scared to touch the cards again. All she could do was stand and stare at the table with one hand on the photo frame and the other clasped tightly to the locket around her neck.

*

Helena had been outside the church for twenty minutes and had finally resorted to removing the offending footwear. Sitting on the low wall she enjoyed the soothing coolness of the pavement under her feet. She listened to the hidden sounds of the night. Enthralled, she watched bats as they flew around the belfry. She was enjoying the peaceful serenity of the night. It wasn't often she got the chance to just to sit still and enjoy the moment. With a husband, two children and a job, Helena had little time for herself.

Sighing, she knew it was time to go home to Jimmy, it was past midnight and he'd be waiting up for her as he always did. Stupidly she had forgotten to bring her phone with her, so she couldn't even call to let him know she was on her way. She gathered up her shoes and despite the cold pavement beneath her feet, set off barefoot, childishly swinging her shoes in her fingers.

*

Jack had left the long country road behind him. After passing through numerous villages he finally found himself in a sprawling town. The roads were completely deserted, and he was able to traverse the suburban streets to the town's centre unhindered.

Keeping an eye peeled for a lurking police car, Jack took another swig from the bottle before wedging it back between his legs. The numbness had made its way into every bone and muscle and the light from the street lamps blurred into a bright white haze. The hurt and depression had subsided and he was left with a sense of numbness, inner peace and calm.

Jack turned a corner into a side street. He hadn't been to this town before and he appreciated its quaintness. Old style houses lined the pavement with neat organised gardens, well-tended trees, shrubs and flowers. The people who lived here cared; it was clean, tidy and well looked after. It showed that they loved where they lived. He wished he and Nikki could have lived in a place like this, but that life was as dead and unobtainable as she was.

Jack was still mulling over the past and trying to light another cigarette as an animal ran across the road in front of him. The frightened mammal's eyes flashed a luminous green as it stared at the hulk of metal bearing down upon it. Swerving erratically, Jack narrowly managed to miss the creature. It was a lucky night for the fox, which ran for cover into a nearby garden as Jack breathed a sigh of relief. He felt dampness on his jeans and, glancing down, realised he'd spilled his bourbon for the sake of avoiding the mammal. In vain he tried to brush the excess liquid away, whilst fumbling to re-cap the bottle to avoid further waste of his precious alcohol.

*

Helena stepped blindly into the road humming her favourite song. Jimmy loved it too and it had unofficially become 'their song' over the years. Strange that she should think of it now. She smiled as she felt a chill in the air. Autumn was swiftly turning to winter. It wouldn't be long before ice appeared to cover puddles and flakes of shimmering powder fell from the sky to dust the world a clean bright white. Her favourite season was fast approaching and she couldn't wait for long dark nights, roaring fires, snow and Christmas. Oh how she loved Christmas!

A screech of tyres stirred Helena from her thoughts and she saw a car swerving wildly in the road, narrowly missing a frightened fox. She breathed with relief as the animal safely scuttled into a garden.

Suddenly, reality hit her. The vehicle was close. Far too close. It was heading straight for her at a speed that was excessively fast. Her brain urged her to run but it was already too late. The vehicle was too quick.

Helena stared at the driver in bewilderment, as everything became slow motion. He wasn't even looking at the road, then, at the last moment, he lifted his head and his shocked and scared eyes locked with hers. Horror etched itself upon both of their faces and there was a brief spark of connection before the sickening sound of metal crunching into breaking bones engulfed them both.

Helena's body flew into the air and she knew in an instant that it was over. Everything fleetingly rippled and she saw Corinne standing next to the fireplace, holding her locket in her hand, her face etched with worry. It disappeared to be replaced by a final vision of Jimmy and her children's faces, making her feel at peace. She was barely able to utter, "I love you" before everything turned black and her fragile body thudded to the road.

Bones shattering.

Skin bruising.

Blood spilling.

Life escaping.

FOUR

Jack tried to brake, honest to God he did. The creature had been one thing, and had scared the shit out of him, but he hadn't expected a woman to step into the road from nowhere, especially at this time of night. The car had skidded violently, brakes and tyres smoking and screeching, before finally hitting her. He had been powerless. The crunch of breaking bone and metal revolted him, and the taste of bile rose to mix with the stale taste of tobacco and alcohol. The girl flew into the air and bounced off the bonnet before landing on the road close to the car, like a battered rag doll discarded by a petulant child. Jack could only stare in horror, his limbs frozen in shock. Despite trying he just couldn't move, he could barely utter a breath.

He sat motionless in the vehicle for a few minutes before eventually setting foot outside, he already knew she was dead; he could see just from looking at her. He had taken a life, turning a bad day into something ultimately much worse. Shaking, he knelt over the body. Brushing a stray hair from the beautiful face, his worst fears confirmed. What had been vivid cerulean blue eyes were now becoming lifeless and glazed, as the colour dulled with every passing second. A trickle of blood seeped from the corner of her mouth, staining her otherwise perfect pale skin. Her body lay twisted and shattered, and a pair of shoes lay abandoned in the road.

What an utter waste.

Clutched in the girl's dead fingers was a silver locket, the chain snapped and tangled. Taking it from her, he glanced at the beautiful face again, running his finger down her cheek, before turning his back. He climbed into his car, trying hard not to vomit. He needed to get away. He had done a terrible, terrible thing and he needed to flee the scene as quickly as possible. Back in the driver's seat he took a reassuring slug of bourbon before leaving the trail of destruction for someone else to find.

*

Corinne was motionless by the fireplace. Her

hand gripped the photo frame so hard that her knuckles had turned white. Corinne had felt Helena's pain and knew she was dead. A tear slid down her cheek and all she could do was utter her beloved sister's name. Blinking back the sting of further tears, her mind played out endless images: running hand in hand with Helena across the school playground; swinging on the swings at the park, each pushing the other higher and higher; blowing out candles on a brightly coloured iced birthday cake, inscribed with their names. All were memories, now lost to the past and Corinne felt completely empty, as though a part of herself perished along with her sister.

The room was airless and still, candles sputtered, nearing their end and the fire extinguished itself in the grate. The tarot spread remained where it was, the unused cards face down on the table, unread.

*

Jack could barely steer the car in a straight line and the rain that had suddenly begun to fall had made the road ahead slick and unsteady. The combination of shock fuelled with alcohol made his hands shake violently. Everything was a blur: the accident, where he was and where he was heading. He had no idea what to do now. He should have reported the accident straight away, he should have stayed with her, and he should have left the locket behind for her family. But he hadn't. Why was that?

Something had taken hold of him, forcing him to act out and do things he would never considered doing before, and now the very worst had happened. He had taken a life he had no right to take, and an innocent girl was dead. He had stolen her locket and was nothing more than a common criminal.

He was a murderer and a thief.

Driving silently through the town, he considered his next move. The darkness of the night smothered him, not even the light from intermittent street lamps helped; they looked ethereal and ghostly, the yellowing light bleeding into the night. He should leave, get as far away as possible, as quickly as possible, but he couldn't. Something was forcing him to stay. He felt a need to hang around, to face up to his responsibilities. He would find somewhere to stop, get some rest and deal with the chaos when he had sobered up and had a clearer head. A few miles on he spied a hostel and checked in, ignoring the wary looks from the receptionist. Once the door was shut behind him, Jack surrendered himself to the dark, dank room, and the lingering stale smells of previous occupants. Despite the bed being lumpy and uncomfortable, sleep came quickly, fuelled by the alcohol that still coursed through his veins. But it was a fitful night filled with repetitive nightmares of lingering death.

*

Eventually Corinne found herself sitting on the bottom step of the hallway staircase. In the dim light she fiddled with her locket staring at the front door, waiting desperately for the knock that she knew was coming but that took an eternity to arrive. She already knew it would be the police and she allowed the officers to enter the house. They guided her back to the stairs making her sit down before confirming the worst.

Helena had been killed in a hit-and-run.

Corinne felt the final break in her heart. Her sister had died alone and the person responsible hadn't even stayed to report the accident, it had been a routine police patrol that had discovered her. Corinne tried her best to listen to what the officer said, but her mind was dragged elsewhere.

Jimmy.

Oh god, Jimmy and the children.

Jimmy had lost his wife and the children,

their mother. They would be hurting and she should go to them. She needed to go to them. They were her only family now and they needed her.

Once the police had done all they could, they left Corinne to the solitude of her hurt and grief. She sat on the stairs holding the locket in her hand, shedding tears for the sister she loved so very much. The sister she would never see, speak to or laugh with again. Corinne couldn't imagine life without her. It took a while to pull herself together enough to stand, but after wiping her eyes and taking a few deep breaths, she extinguished the candles and damped down the fire before setting off to Helena's house.

*

Jimmy's hands shook with shock. He had been sitting there, unable to move, ever since the police had visited him to break the terrible news. He was trying his best not to wake the children, but his sobs echoed around the large high-ceilinged living room.

He couldn't believe it. His precious, beautiful Helena, light of his life, was dead. He tried his best to take in the news, but it just wouldn't sink in. He would never again see her walk through the door, never again see her smiling face as she praised the children, never again see that playful glint in her eye as she seductively kissed him, before leading him up the stairs to their bedroom room to hold each other tight and make love.

The loss was unbearable, as though his heart had been torn from his chest and ripped into tiny pieces. He had yet to tell the children their mummy was never coming home and he dreaded it. How was he going explain that their mummy would never walk them to school again, or tuck them into bed and read them a story? How much heartbreak could one man suffer? Losing his wife was one thing but causing his children life-long hurt would be something else, and he wasn't sure he would cope with it very well.

The sudden sound of a key in the front door lock made him look up. As it swung open his heart leapt, and he hurriedly ran to the hallway wiping the salty tears from his face. Disbelief etched itself across his face as he watched the figure walk through the open doorway.

His heart skipped a beat; Helena was alive! The police had gotten it wrong!

She ran over to Jimmy, threw her arms around him, hugged him tightly and whispered his name. Sitting on the stairs she held him close and rocked him gently. But the elation that had briefly overwhelmed him disappeared. The smell wasn't Helena, the voice not hers either, and the tone was edged with sympathy, not love.

Corinne.

Quietly they sat, with only the continual howl of the wind and patter of rain against the windows breaking through the silence that pervaded the house. The in-laws remained seated on the stairs sharing their grief. Corinne was thankful to hold on to a small part of her sister's world that still existed, the husband and home that had been her everyday life. Jimmy clung resentfully to the mirror image of Helena, a woman who was identical in every way to his wife, but who wasn't, and never would be her.

FIVE

The day was cold and misty. Rain had fallen
steadily overnight, drenching thirsty plants and
trees, leaving behind fresh puddles that littered
roads and pavements. The wind whistled
through the trees, detaching leaves, and sending
them on a chaotic skyward journey. They flew in
all directions eventually coming to a standstill in
small piles where they briefly rested before being
lifted aloft once more to be carried away on the
breeze.

A solitary gravedigger, wrapped in warm
clothes to protect against the elements, was hard
at work in the churchyard. He was in the final
stages of digging a fresh grave that would be
filled later in the day. It was cold for excavating
and he was finding it hard going. His job was

always difficult, as he knew most people who lived in town, but this time it was different. He had known the deceased very well. He'd gone to the same school as her and been friends with her husband growing up. It was hard when one of your own friends died. It made you think about your own life and mortality.

The entire town had a subdued atmosphere which would remain a while longer, until the happy spark of life that everyone had known and loved so well was laid to rest. Many of the town's inhabitants had known the twins from birth, and the callous hit-and-run death of one of them a few weeks before had shocked the community to its very core. What upset them more was the suspicion that a cold-hearted murderer could be living amongst them. Distrust was rife and the town's cracks were starting to show. They needed to stick together in times like these.

*

Corinne had appropriately dressed herself in black. Perched upon her head was a small black hat with a thin veil that partially covered her face. An unsettling reflection stared back at her from the mirror: darkness circled her eyes, and she looked pale and gaunt. Most notably, her normally brilliant cerulean eyes had lost their life and sparkle; the blueness had dulled, like the sky losing its colour to a grey overcast day. Grief had hit her hard and the signs were all too visible.

The tarot spread from the night Helena died still sat undisturbed on the table behind her, the cards taunting her each time she looked at them. Dust had settled upon them and she knew she should put them back in their box, but couldn't bear to touch them, at least not until after the funeral. She couldn't explain why; she just felt she needed to leave them where they were until Helena was finally buried.

Adjusting her clothing one last time, she glanced lovingly at the photo of her and her sister. Corinne missed her so much and the grief was eating her from the inside out, making her exhausted and miserable. She could barely eat, sleep had eluded her since the accident, and it was beginning to take its toll on her, both mentally and physically. She extinguished the sole burning candle next to the photograph; her own silent, daily, mark of respect to her sister.

It was time to go and lay Helena to rest.

*

Jack was sitting in a café at a scuffed and stained plastic table that had seen better days. A strong black coffee was cradled in his hand. It was the first sober day he'd had since the accident and today of all days he wanted to stay that way out of respect. Rather than running away, he'd stayed in the hostel, going over the accident in his head, trying to make sense of what had happened, of why he had acted the way he had and why he was so reluctant to leave. In the end he had decided to wait around for the funeral. He was filled with guilt and felt the least he could do was stay to pay his respects; he owed the girl that much. It hadn't been difficult to find out the details. Talk of her death was everywhere. It seemed many knew her and mourned for her.

The clock on the café wall crept closer to one o'clock, and Jack ordered another coffee. Opening his tightly clutched hand, he took another look at the necklace. A thin silver chain and locket containing a photograph of the girl lay in his palm. Jack still had no idea why he'd taken it, but he had, and he had looked at it almost every hour of every day since the accident, as if trying to soften his guilt somehow.

Unthreading the locket from the tangled and broken chain, he carefully placed it in his jacket pocket before discarding the chain. Turning his head, he stared out the window. The funeral procession was passing as expected. The hearse containing the coffin was decked out with three simple floral tributes that simply read *wife*, *mummy* and *sister*. The sight of it made him go cold. He was utterly ashamed of what he had done, and felt he was no better than the person who'd killed Nikki; a common, cowardly criminal. How dare he sit here and pretend to care when he had caused so much pain and despair to so many people? He was a hypocrite, talking to shop owners and bar keepers about the terrible accident, speculating who had caused such hurt and deceit in the midst of their community, when all along he wanted to stand in the street and scream, "It was me!"

The family car followed the hearse, and a woman in the rear seat locked eyes with him for the briefest of moments. Jack's brain was instantly hit with a flashback of the accident, and he was shocked to see the victim's ghost staring straight back at him.

How could that be?

Reaching for the locket, he opened it and the realisation hit him; the woman in the car and the woman in the locket were one and the same.

Twins.

She looked so alone and completely lost, and now he understood why.

As the cars passed by, inching ever closer to their final destination, he pushed away his coffee, threw some money on the table and left the café.

*

The funeral was low-key at Jimmy's request, with only family and a few close friends in attendance. Despite his wishes, locals had gathered outside of the church to watch the cortege arrive and to pay their own respects. Once the service had been conducted, Corinne, Jimmy and the two children followed the priest to the freshly dug grave, each desperately holding on to the other for support. Standing next to the dark coffin-shaped hole that was to be Helena's final resting place, they listened to the priest say his piece.

As much as she tried to stay strong for Jimmy and the children, Corinne could feel the tears falling, but was incapable of stopping them. She was completely numb. More than that, she was exhausted. She was broken-hearted at losing her sister, her twin. She no longer felt whole and never would again. Corinne caught sight of the children standing proudly next to their father, little Freddie wearing smart trousers and a jumper under his coat and Rosie with her best dress, topped off with a woolly hat and scarf. Corinne was surprised that two children under the age of ten could behave so well at such a solemn occasion. Helena would have been so proud of them. As the coffin was slowly lowered to the depths, her fingers tightly clasped the locket that hung around her neck. She gripped it so hard that the delicate silver chain snapped sending the locket tumbling to the ground.

Jimmy was well aware that his sister-in-law was falling apart, and knew it was just as hard on her as it was on him. The twins had lost their parents a few years before, and had no other family. They were everything to each other. *Had* been everything to each other. He watched Corinne as she absentmindedly fingered the locket, one of a matching pair he had bought them one Christmas. It had become their favourite item of jewellery and they always wore them. As she continued to fiddle, the delicate chain snapped and it tumbled to the ground. Without a second thought Jimmy reached down into the damp, green blades to find it, wiping away the morning dew before pressing it into her hand, knowing how precious it was. Carefully, Corinne placed it in her bag, before taking a handful of soft brown earth, and sprinkling it onto the coffin below. After the service they each shook the priest's hand and watched him depart, his robes flowing wildly behind him collecting dew from the damp ground.

Corinne, Jimmy and the children stood

silently next to the grave, unable to move or say their final goodbyes. This is what life had come to: Helena was gone and husband and sister were now alone. Corinne knew she could always talk to Jimmy, but her sister, friend, partner in crime and confidante was lost to her forever. Never again would she see Helena's beautiful smile, hear her laugh, see those vibrant blue eyes light up with mischief, watch as she entertained friends and family, or open her heart to Corinne to talk about things that only a sister could help with.

Corinne had lost everything the moment the car ploughed into her. She had felt Helena's pain as her body died, pain that remained with her, waking her at night in a cold sweat, creeping up on her when she least expected it, and it would remain so until the day Corinne herself was finally laid to rest alongside her.

Suddenly aware of people passing on condolences, Corinne shook herself from her melancholy. She tried to listen to the kindly faces, to take in what they were saying but all she heard was a jumble of words. She was exhausted and just went through the motions of accepting the platitudes from the well-wishers. It was hard and she found it nearly impossible to speak. What could she possibly say? Finally, as the mourners began to drift away, Jimmy draped his arm around her shoulder. He pulled her to him and hugged her tightly. She closed her eyes, gratefully accepting the comfort. When the moment passed he said his own farewell to his dead wife and departed with the children, leaving Corinne alone in the chill of the day, staring at the mound of fresh earth that was her sister's new home.

Standing motionless, Corinne allowed thoughts of their lives to whirl through her head: the fun they'd had climbing the old gnarled tree at the foot of the garden, throwing rotten apples at the neighbourhood boys as they passed, swimming in the lake in the summer, running through the grass in the bright hot sun. When they got older they chose which of the neighbourhood boys they would sneak out for and kiss under the light of the moon. They had always joked about getting old, saying that they would end up sitting on a battered old porch swing watching their great-grandchildren play, laughing and gossiping about all the things they had done in their lives. But now it would never happen, and the thought of that completely broke Corinne's heart.

SIX

Leaning against an ancient lichen-covered gravestone, Jack watched her. She must be freezing by now. The miserable weather had turned, clouds had begun to part and a weak sun now shone, but it was still bitterly cold. He could see the frigid air eating through layers of clothes making her visibly shake, but she just remained staring at the grave. It was as if she had been turned to stone, forced to stay in the graveyard as a reminder of the lost beauty that lay beneath her feet. He walked over to stand by her side, no longer caring if he interrupted a private moment. He needed to talk to her.

"You okay?" He asked quietly, not wanting to scare her.

Corinne was instantly pulled from her trance

by the gentleness of a voice she didn't recognise.

Her response was barely a whisper.

"Hit and run. Why do people do it?"

Jack felt the guilt wash over him and his hands became clammy despite the temperature. How could he stand there and pretend to care when the whole mess was his fault? He was a murderer. What was he even doing here? Was he really that sick and twisted? He should walk away, leave her to the grief and suffering he'd caused, but he couldn't. Something stopped him. He was drawn to her. He could see that she was a mess and needed to be looked after. It was something he wanted to see through, even if it seemed like madness.

"Were you related or just a friend?" Jack asked, knowing the answer before she gave it.

"She was my sister. My twin sister."

Corrine looked up at him as if seeing him for the first time. Surprise caught her. He was a good-looking man, if in a slightly dark, moody, mysterious sort of way. He was wearing blue jeans, black shirt, leather jacket and biker boots. His mid-length scruffy hair brushed the collar of the shirt, falling over his sharp, dark, piercing eyes, eyes that glinted like steel in the crisp daylight. A faint inviting aroma of tobacco and aftershave lingered about him. Whoever he was, she liked him.

"Did you know her? Is that why you're here?"

He shook his head, unsure of how to answer. What could he possibly say?

"No, I was passing through to another grave. I saw you on your own, and you looked upset."

"I'm fine... Sorry, I don't know your name."

"Jack. My name is Jack."

"Jack. Well thank you, but I really am okay."

The conversation with Jack brought her back to reality, making her realise how cold it was. She could feel the damp chill that had seeped through her clothing and the numbness that enveloped her hands and feet. She had been there for far too long, and it was time to leave. Smiling weakly at Jack she turned and walked away.

Jack followed. He wasn't ready to let her go yet.

"Do you need a ride? My car's close by."

"No thanks, I'd rather walk."

Corinne ceased walking for the briefest of moments and turned to face him. She didn't want to be rude. Despite not knowing him, he had been kind and honest. That was what she craved instead of subject avoidance and sympathy like everyone else was giving her. For some reason she liked this man and felt a strong connection to him. There was no harm in being polite. She smiled at him.

"But thank you Jack. I appreciate the offer. I hope to see you around."

*

As she walked away, Jack leant against a gravestone watching her. Her beauty had floored him and he had found it difficult to look at her without staring like a ridiculous schoolboy. He took out his cigarettes, lit one and pulled deeply on it. As captivating as she was it didn't make things any better. In fact, seeing the utter destruction he'd left behind only made him feel much worse. He was in turmoil. He wanted desperately to get to know her better, but he had committed a grave crime and knew that the right thing to do would be to hand himself in to the police, to own up, to give the family closure, but something was stopping him. He feared for his own fate and just couldn't do it. He didn't want to spend the rest of his life in prison. Funny that, considering he had spent a lot of time recently wishing he could just disappear off the face of the earth.

Maybe he wanted to live after all.

*

The wake was a simple affair, held at Helena and Jimmy's home. The house was large and white, with a bright red front door flanked by two mock columns. A large front lawn was framed by overhanging trees and bushes that enticed a multitude of birds hunting insects. A driveway with room for more than one car ran the length of the garden and house. Today it was full. Despite the freezing weather, Jimmy sat on the front step, staring at the garden that had been Helena's haven. His tie lay crumpled on the ground next to him, his shirt collar was unbuttoned, and he was gripping a cup of strong black coffee in an effort to keep his hands warm. He had felt trapped and harangued inside, and needed some time to himself. His home was filled with family and well-wishers and the front step was the only place where he found some time alone. He was trying to be strong for his children, but the grief was eating him up from the inside out, he was completely lost without Helena. He missed her terribly and wished that he could do something to change what had happened, but he couldn't. This was their life now. He was a widower and the children were motherless. It wasn't supposed to be like this and it left him feeling lost, miserable and very lonely.

Corinne opened the front door, letting the chill of the day in. She had been looking for Jimmy for ten minutes and was worried as to where he'd gone. It wasn't good for him to be alone for too long. Closing the door behind her to keep the house warm, she took a seat on the cold step next to him, pulling her wrap tightly about her shoulders. They had barely spoken since Helena's death, and Corinne knew he was hurting just as much as she. He had lost the love of his life.

"I'm so sorry Jimmy."

"It's okay... We'll be fine."

"You know I'm always here, if you or the kids need me. All you need to do is call me."

Corinne put her arm around him and hugged him but, unlike the hug at the churchyard, Jimmy pulled away. He had found it more and more difficult during the wake. He kept seeing his wife's double walking through the house, hugging his children, talking with friends and it hurt deeply. To him, the wrong sister had died. He didn't hate Corinne, but her being alive was a stark reminder of all that he'd lost. He needed time, he needed to grieve, and he couldn't do that with Corinne around.

"We'll be fine." Then after a long pause, Jimmy sighed and said, "It's hard being around you Corinne. All I see when I look at you is Helena: her face, her eyes, her hair. But you're not her. She's lying six feet under and you're still here, a reminder of everything I've lost. It's so unfair. I need space Corinne, time and space. Maybe it's best if you stay away for a while. I know that sounds harsh, but it's how I feel. I'm sorry."

Gathering up his tie, Jimmy stood, turned his back on his sister-in-law, and entered the warmth of the house. Left outside alone in the cold, Corinne felt the tears fall. She couldn't help looking like Helena. She had no choice; they'd been born that way. She knew Jimmy was distraught and would probably get over it in time, but she was hurting too, and he and the children were all she had left, her only link to her sister, she couldn't lose them too. As she cried his words echoed around her head, they had cut through her like a knife. The wound would eventually heal, but the scar would remain forever.

SEVEN

The bar's interior was dark, gloomy and quiet. Jack was thankful. The last thing he wanted was to have to make small talk with some drunken bar hopper who was drowning their sorrows after a row with their wife. His stool was pulled up to the long bar. A large glass of bourbon rested untouched on the wooden surface. The drink teased him, called him, begged to be drunk. Jack couldn't stop thinking about the dead girl's sister. Despite her beauty she had looked thin, tired, gaunt and full of un-ending grief, and it was all his fault. The look in her eyes haunted him almost as much as her dead sister's had. They were so alike, it was if the dead girl's ghost had risen and come back to torment him. Was this what karma looked and felt like?

As he toyed with the glass the jukebox churned out tune after miserable tune. He could tell by the selections that it was the pretty blonde bar tender's choice; sappy girl songs that reminded him of Nikki, the sort that she would have loved and sung at him with those bright mischievous eyes, before holding and kissing him, running her hands through his hair and...

Stop!

It was no good going over this again. He had to let it go. Nikki was dead. As dead as the girl he'd killed. There was no way he could change the past, so why did his mind keep sending him back there?

Lifting the glass he took a swig, feeling the liquid burn as it went down. It was a welcome relief. He'd hated abstaining, but he relished the taste once more and it went down all too easily.

The jukebox finished its current refrain, briefly submitting the room to silence before clicking over to a new track. Jack recognised the opening bars and froze, his mind instantly returning to the moment of Helena's impact with his car. It was as though the world was taunting him, leaving small reminders of what he'd done, everywhere he went. Quickly he downed the rest of the glass before leaving the bar. The song was too much, a memory that was too intense, it made him feel sick and uneasy. He had to get away to the one remaining place he felt safe.

Climbing into his car he sped off, another unknown drive ahead of him.

*

The house was quieter now. Remaining guests had passed on their condolences and left the family in peace. Corinne silently made her way around the rooms collecting empty glasses, plates and cups before loading them into the dishwasher. She gathered up the rubbish, and threw it into bin bags, before cleaning kitchen surfaces, leaving everything as tidy as possible. Pausing at the living room door, she leaned against the frame watching Jimmy and her niece and nephew. They had fallen fast asleep, huddled up on the sofa, and looked so peaceful that she hadn't the heart to wake them to say goodbye. Quietly, she crept over to them, and planted the gentlest of kisses on each of their foreheads. Without looking back, she pulled her coat around her shoulders, grabbed her bag and left the confines of her sister's house, stepping out into the cold.

Corinne ambled through the streets, desperate for fresh air after the heat and claustrophobia of the house and its guests. It was still cold, and the sun had begun to wane once more, so she pulled her coat tightly around her to keep out as much of the chilly air as possible. Jimmy's words still stung. Helena would have been horrified to see them so strained. All she could do was give him time and hope that he'd eventually come round. She loved them too much to lose them as well.

Mulling over past memories, she walked the cold and damp streets. Stray leaves that had managed to make it into the early winter months and other debris littered the pavements and road gutters, occasionally carried along by the wind to form small piles that would be swept up the following day by council workers. Corinne favoured this time of the year. Most people she knew hated it but she found solace in the drama of the weather, the bleakness of the season and the stripping back of the trees until they were nothing but bare branches. Corinne enjoyed the anticipation of the forthcoming cold snap, filled with ice and snow that would blanket everything and sometimes last for months. Yes, she loved late autumn and the bleakness of winter that followed.

She turned a corner and found herself on the street where her sister had died. She and Helena had loved this part of town, and it held so many special memories. It was the route they had always taken from their parents' house to the family church, which stood proudly near the accident site. It was sad that Helena had been killed in an area of town they held most dear. When she reached the church, Corinne stopped and leaned on the low wall to remove an irritating stone from her shoe.

*

Jack had been driving for hours. He wasn't going anywhere in particular, but driving was his escape. It was hard to stay in the hostel staring blankly at a TV screen. He knew that he should leave now that the funeral was over. This was not his town, there was nothing to keep him here and every day he remained he was at risk of getting caught. But something was forcing him to stay, an unknown power, taking over, forcing him to do its bidding. All he could think about was the dead woman's sister. She crept into his dreams every night and refused to leave him alone. All he wanted to do was see her again and it scared him.

Turning a corner he found himself in the street where the accident had happened. He hadn't meant to come here, but it was as though an unknown force had guided him there, to remind him of his worst nightmare; a nightmare that lived with him and never went away.

As he reached the church, he almost choked on his cigarette. He really was being taunted. There she stood. The dead woman's sister.

He knew that he should keep driving, leave the town and never come back, but he couldn't; something stopped him, it was as if he was being drawn to her. Somehow he needed to make amends, although how he might do this was completely eluding him.

Pulling the car to the kerb, he wound down the window.

"Hello there."

Hearing a voice, Corrine looked up and stared blankly at the man leaning out of a car window. He seemed to be directing his conversation at her. There was something attractively familiar about him, but she just couldn't put her finger on it.

"Sorry, do I know you?"

"We met at your sister's funeral. I'm Jack."

She remembered him now, the man who had spoken to her at the graveside. The handsome man with wild eyes and an inviting smell of tobacco and aftershave. The thought brought a fleeting smile to her lips.

"Jack, of course," she shivered with cold.

"You're freezing. Do you want a ride

somewhere?"

"No I'm alright, but thanks for the offer."

The wind picked up and whistled down the street, collecting more debris from the gutter, flinging it in all directions as it went. It tugged at Corinne's coat and she shivered again, unable to get warm. Her fingers were too numb to do up the remaining buttons, and she realised her teeth were chattering.

Jack climbed out of the car, walked over, and leaned against the wall next to her. He motioned to his car. "Come on, get in before you freeze. What are you going to do, stay here all night?"

She knew he was right. She was just being stubborn because she had poor social skills and hated meeting new people, especially handsome men that intrigued her and stirred feelings within her that she hadn't felt in a very long time.

"Thank you, Jack. I appreciate the offer," she paused, unsure of what to say next, before remembering that she knew his name but he had no clue of hers.

"I'm Corinne, by the way."

"Hi there Corinne," he said, smiling, but she noticed that the smile never reached his eyes. A mystery. "Now come on, get in the car and let me take you home."

Jack took hold of her hand and put his arm around her in an effort to help her to the waiting vehicle, suddenly without warning she went limp in his arms, falling like a rag doll to the pavement.

EIGHT

Corinne felt completely adrift. Day had changed to night in an instant and her body was no longer her own. Dizziness overwhelmed her and she tried to get her bearings. She was in a street, but where? Spinning around she saw the church and familiarity washed over her. She knew where she was now.

Suddenly, to her left, she saw the great hulk of car speeding along the road, the headlights too bright, blinding her, and the engine too loud, deafening her. It was like she had been transported to another time and place. Ahead of her, she saw Helena crossing the road, singing to herself, her favourite sandals swinging loosely from her delicate fingers. The car was heading straight for her and Corinne watched helplessly as it hit her. She held out her arm trying to reach for her sister. She opened her mouth to scream but nothing came out. Corinne gulped for air feeling like she was drowning and then blackness enveloped her once more.

In the depth of dark shadows she heard a voice, it was insistent, calling her name but she felt trapped in a murky fog. She listened for it and there it was again, her name, echoing in the dark. She followed the voice as it slowly pulled her back to the surface of reality.

"Corinne!" Jack was trying with all of his might to bring her back to consciousness, "Corinne, talk to me!"

Finding herself slumped against the wall, Corinne tried to raise her head. She still felt dizzy, sick and slightly disoriented. Breathing deeply, she concentrated on helping the feelings pass. Eventually she opened her eyes, as the uneasy feelings finally dissipated. It was daylight, and there was no sign of Helena or the car. What the hell had happened?

"Are you feeling alright?"

"I think so. What happened?"

"I'm not sure. I went to help you to the car and the next minute you were deadweight in my arms. I think you fainted."

Corinne was shaken. It looked like her

visions were returning with a vengeance. They were becoming more common, as though she were being forced to live out her sister's final moments, but she had no idea why. She had always had the ability to see things before they happened, but it had never been this strong before, and she had always seen the future, not the past. It scared and unnerved her. It was like Helena was talking to her from beyond the grave, but it wasn't possible. Was it?

She had to think about it sensibly, but she was too tired and confused to be reasonable about anything right now. Fatigue was making her so confused. She could put it down to not eating any food since breakfast, and the stress of everything that had happened. Perhaps it was just one of those strange dreams you got when you fainted. Helena had been on her mind and she was at the scene of the accident after all. She was too tired to think about it now, and needed to just get into the car and go home.

"Come on let me help you," Jack reached forward to help Corinne to her feet, but she declined, using the wall to help her up. Slowly, step by step, she made her way to the car under her own steam. Jack shrugged, following in her wake. Corinne climbed into the passenger seat, and Jack closed the door. The interior of the vehicle was spacious and she felt insignificant in the large soft leather of the passenger seat. The car smelled like its owner; a mild musky mix, pleasant but not overpowering. Jack climbed in, started the engine and pulled away in silence. Corinne kept her eyes on the passing suburban sprawl not knowing what to say until finally Jack broke the chasm of silence between them.

"Where do you live?"

"Main Street. You know how to get there?"

"Yes."

Silence returned once more, descending like a cloud. Jack concentrated on the road as Corinne continued to gaze out of the window. The sky had darkened and street lamps were flickering on. The day was coming to an end. She spoke only as they reached Main Street, to tell him which house was hers. Jack pulled the car to the kerb and she climbed out, firmly shutting the door behind her.

He lowered the window and a rush of cold air washed over him.

"Goodnight Corinne."

"Thank you, Jack."

She turned, climbed the front steps, and paused for a moment to look back. What was it about him, she thought, entering the house, closing the door behind her. She threw her coat and bag over the banister before picking up a book of matches, walking through the safe haven of her home lighting candles as she went.

*

Jack sat in the car. The engine was still running and emitted a low throaty grumble. Lighting a cigarette, he watched the house with intrigue; Corinne was a mystery. He had felt the softness of her skin when he'd taken her hand in his and smelt the faint scent of flowers about her as he'd cradled her in her arms after falling to the pavement. He had realised in that moment, whilst holding her, how desperately he wanted to get to know her, but in the car she had put up a wall, and he'd had no idea what to say to her. Outwardly it was as if she didn't want to talk to anyone, so he'd just left her to her own devices. He knew he should walk away but part of him wanted to spend time with her, to be part of her life. He wanted to know more about her sister, the woman he'd killed, and the only way to do that was to get to know Corinne. He knew he was playing a dangerous game, but since when had that ever stopped him from doing anything?

Light illuminated the front room and he saw Corinne cross to the mantelpiece. She lit another candle before lifting a photo frame that sat atop the wood. As she held it tightly to her chest she began to cry, her shoulders heaving great sobs, and she had to grip the mantelpiece to steady herself.

Jack discarded his cigarette, flicking it to the pavement. Reaching over to the glove box, he removed a bottle. Turning off the engine he climbed from the vehicle before mounting the steps in one leap.

*

It still amazed Corinne how waves of grief could suddenly wash over her like an all-enveloping tidal wave, dragging with them countless memories, both good and bad, debris that was left floating around her brain in a tangle of murky water.

A sudden knock startled her. She placed the photo frame back on the mantelpiece, and wiped her eyes with her dress sleeve in an effort to remove the salted tears. Corinne opened the door to find Jack leaning against the frame.

"I thought you'd left?"

"You looked upset," he said, lifting the bottle, "Want a drink?"

Corinne needed company, someone to help pull her from the edge of the pit of despair she was standing on. She wanted someone to talk to, someone who didn't know her, someone who wouldn't judge. She wanted someone to just sit and listen and make her feel like they were there for her and cared. He seemed the perfect choice.

"Come in."

Jack entered, following her through the dim candlelit house to the front room. He stopped in surprise at the bleak, minimal scene before him. Two chairs sat either side of an open hearth, which Corinne was now knelt in front of. She patiently lit the kindling, building up logs around it to catch the flame. As she toiled he continued to take in his surroundings. A small table sat in front of the fire by the chairs, other than that, the room was bare. Even the floorboards were on show, with only a small threadbare rug to break the uniformity of the wood. Jack wondered how someone could live in a house so devoid of comfort and character.

Finally Corinne stood, brushing dust and ash from her hands before lighting the few remaining candles on the mantelpiece. She left the room for a moment. While she was gone, Jack crossed to the chairs and took a seat in one of them, feeling the heat of the fire warm him. It was a welcome relief.

Corinne returned with two glasses and placed them on the table. Taking the bottle from Jack she poured a few fingers of the golden liquid into the tumblers, before putting the bottle on the table. She passed one of the glasses to him, sipping from her own as she sat opposite. Jack slugged back the bourbon before turning his attention to the photo frame on the mantelpiece.

"Is that you and your sister?" he asked, breaking the silence.

Corinne glanced over her shoulder at the image that caused her an equal measure of pain and pleasure.

"Yes. It was taken on our birthday two years ago."

"Which one are you?"

"On the left."

Corinne closely studied the man before her, the good-looking stranger who always seemed to be there when she needed him. But he was a man who she knew so little about, and had a guarded air about him. He had turned up in her life one day, completely unexpected, and always seemed to be there at every turn. Why was that?

"Who are you Jack?"

"Who am I?"

Corinne laughed, "It's not a trick question. I just don't know anything about you. You suddenly appeared in my life, and seem to keep turning up when I need rescuing, and I have no idea who you are or why you're here. You know about my tragedy, my sister, and you're here in my house making up your mind about the type of person I am from what you can see before you, and yet I know nothing at all about you, other than you drive that monster of a car, smoke and drink bourbon. So, who are you?"

Jack reached for the bottle to top up his glass.

"Another drink?"

She shrugged and held out the glass for him. He was deliberately being evasive. She tried to read his face as he slowly re-filled her glass, but it was impassive.

"Were you and your sister close?"

"You're changing the subject."

"Maybe I am. Maybe it's because I'm not ready to talk about myself yet."

She sighed and swallowed back some of the liquor.

"Okay, if you're asking if my sister and I have...I'm sorry...had that 'twin thing' then yes, we did, so that made us very close indeed. Her name was Helena by the way."

She paused to look at the photograph again, a stray tear escaping, despite her earlier promise not to cry in front of him. She desperately wanted to though, she wanted to cry and scream and lash out, for the loss of her sister and the loss of Jimmy and the children, but however much she wanted to, she just couldn't do it in front of a stranger, especially one who refused to tell her anything about himself.

"Enough about my sister. I asked about *you* Jack."

Corrine stared at him. He wasn't going to have it all his own way, and she wouldn't talk about Helena anymore today. Jack sat there and stared back at her. He wasn't ready to share yet, he had stopped in to help her, not burden her with his own problems.

 Stalemate.

"Well?" Corinne asked again a few minutes later after the silence between them had become unbearable.

Sighing, he knew he was beaten. He topped up his glass again, before swigging back two fingers of the sweet bourbon. He drew another breath and finally spoke.

"There's little to tell. I live on my own and have no family. I love my car, my cigarettes and my alcohol. Sorry to disappoint you Corinne, but I'm a lonely man, with no one to care for, and no one cares for me."

The shutters descended on both sides of the table as they drank, with only the crackling of the open fire and odd hissing of flickering candles breaking the tension. Corinne had had enough and stood, she tipped the glass back, finishing the remainder of her drink in one go.

"Well, thanks for the drink Jack."

It was time for him to leave.

"Are you sure you'll be all right?"

"Yes. I'm sure."

He knew she was lying, but she was already a closed book. He would get nothing further from her tonight. Swilling back the remainder of the bourbon, he placed the empty glass on the table.

"See you Corinne."

After making his way through the gloom of the house, he let himself out. Corinne heard the door close behind him and watched from the window as he climbed into his car and drove away.

Lifting the brown leather-bound book that had been sitting on the mantelpiece, Corinne pulled a chair closer to the table. She opened the book and began to write, recording the events of the day, as she did every day. Today would be no different. As she wrote, her memory danced around, recalling happier times. She sat pouring her heart out on to the paper, tears staining the words so that she could barely read them, writing fast and hard until her hand cramped so much that she could scarcely hold the pen.

NINE

The sun was slowly climbing, casting a luminous glow on the world below, bathing everything in a bright warm light, signalling the start of a new day. The weather had begun to get a little warmer than it had been of late, and the incessant wind that had seeped into bones and hurled debris through the streets had dropped to a mere gentle whisper. It had been a harsh, but beautiful winter and the snow and ice had arrived as predicted, bathing everything in a crisp white glow. Remnants of slushy brown ice that had once been clean white crystals lay in heaps around the town, now quickly melting as spring fast approached.

Corinne stood in the window of her front room staring out at the street beyond. Her stomach was a mass of butterflies and try as she might she couldn't stomach her breakfast so it ended up in the bin.

Downing her coffee she placed the empty cup on the table and went to the mirror in the hallway to set about finishing her make-up. Staring at her reflection she was surprised by what she saw. She looked a lot less tired and drawn than she had in recent months. Her eyes had lost their dark circles and the colour had returned to her cheeks. Overall she was looking much better. Her make-up finished, she pulled on her coat, extinguished the candle that still burned for her sister on a daily basis, and left the house.

*

Sitting on the front step of his house, Jimmy looked worn-out and anxious. He had been waiting for this day. It hadn't come as a surprise, but the last few months had passed so quickly and suddenly it was here. He had spent the previous night tossing and turning, staring at the ceiling re-playing the events of Helena's accident in his head. He still carried the guilt with him daily. He should have gone to collect Helena from her night out, but she had hated him fussing. And yet if he had gone, she wouldn't have walked home on her own and wouldn't have been killed; she would still be here now. He blamed himself and nothing anyone said would make him change how he thought.

Christmas had been unbearable. He and the children had missed her terribly. Helena had always loved it, and the house hadn't been the same without her dancing around the living room wearing tinsel and singing Christmas songs. He had tried to make the day a good one for the children but his attempts were sadly lacking, and it had fallen to his parents to keep the children amused and happy.

He also loathed how he had treated Corinne at the wake. It was the last time he had seen her and he missed her company. Speaking to her that way had been despicable and Helena would have hated him for what he had done. He had tried so many times to contact her to apologise, but each time he tried he hesitated, not able to bring himself to make the call. Too much time had passed and he no longer knew what to say. He didn't know how to make amends; he didn't know how to make it better.

Finally his parents had called her forcing him to talk to her. She had spoken with such love and kindness as though there had never been an issue and he felt nothing but relief. He had his sister-in-law back and the children had their aunt, and he felt much happier for it. He was now sitting and waiting for her to collect him so that they could go and face the final verdict together.

Glancing up, he saw Corinne step from the car waving and smiling broadly. He was pleased to see her and after not seeing her for so long he realised what an idiot he had been. Yes, she and Helena were twins, but if he looked hard enough he could list the many differences between them. Corinne dressed completely differently, and Helena always straightened her hair, whereas Corinne's fell with natural waves. Corinne always wore lots of jewellery, but Helena only wore her wedding band and locket necklace. Corinne's nose was slightly crooked, and Helena was perfect in every way. Their mannerisms were also completely different. He had been such a fool, but as his parents had told him, grief did funny things to people.

He stood and smiled warmly.

*

It seemed like forever since Corinne had seen Jimmy or the children and his words still hurt, but she had learned to live with them. It had been a complete surprise when he'd asked her to go to the inquest with him, awkwardly admitting he needed her support and it was what

Helena would have wanted. She knew it was all down to his parents. She had seen them a few times around town and each time they had apologised profusely for their son's behaviour. In the end it didn't matter how or why he'd contacted her, she was just glad to be able to start getting things back to normal.

Jimmy walked towards her and politely, if awkwardly, opened his arms and hugged her. Gracefully she accepted it.

"I'm so scared," he whispered.

"I know Jimmy. I am too, but it will be okay. It will all be over soon."

They set off in Corinne's car for the short journey to Court. Once they had parked, they entered the building and patiently waited for the session to begin. Nerves affected both of them. Jimmy couldn't sit still and paced the hallway wringing his hands, glancing continually at his watch. Corinne felt sick to the stomach, waves of dread and dizziness washing over her as she tapped her foot on the floor impatiently. It was a relief when they were finally called through.

The inquest lasted for almost four hours, but to Corinne it was a blur. They were presented with aspects of Helena's life, forensic evidence, the accident and how it was perceived by the police to have happened, and other legal jargon that went completely over her head. It seemed, despite a thorough investigation, there were no witnesses, and still no arrests. Corinne barely took in what was being said. The only time she shed a tear was when police photographs of Helena's lifeless body appeared on the screen. They were sickening. Helena's body was twisted and broken, lying on the tarmac in a pool of blood, her eyes dead and glazed. It was not how Corinne wanted to remember her sister, and it was as much as she could do to stay in the room. But stay she did, gripping Jimmy's hand tightly, as he shook with shock.

Once the final verdict was given, they made their way outside and stood at the bottom of the steps, with weak early spring sun shining down upon them.

Jimmy pushed away a few stray tears and said, "An accident. Nothing more, nothing less. How could that be?"

Corinne had expected more, and she felt they had been let down.

"I don't know, but at least we have some idea of what happened and can start getting on with our lives," she said, trying her best to comfort him, knowing it meant little.

"I know, but I'd feel happier if they had actually arrested someone. It seems there's nothing more we can do." He paused before speaking again, "Thank you for coming with me Corinne."

"She was my sister; I'd have been here no matter what. Take care of yourself, Jimmy. You and the children are all that matters now, be strong for them."

"You too. I'll be in touch soon. You should come over, the kids miss you," he paused awkwardly. "So do I."

"I miss you too."

They hugged and Corinne knew he was trying to find some words of apology for the last time they had spoken, but it didn't matter. What he'd said and done today was already enough and she made it easy for him. Pushing back from him she pressed her car keys into his hand.

"Go on, take the car and get back to Freddie and Rosie. I need some air, and it's not too far to walk."

"If you're sure?"

"Yes. I'll pop over and collect the car in the next few days, which means I can see the monsters then," she said with a wide smile.

"Thank you." He gently kissed her on the cheek before walking away.

Corinne was grateful that they had finally started to make amends; she had missed them all so much. She hadn't been lying; she did need the fresh air, and wasn't ready to go back home yet. She had no idea where she was going but she walked through the town's streets, quiet in her own thoughts, mulling over everything that had happened since her sister's death. Over the long winter months, the intense visions had subsided and the grief had waned a little, but it was still there bubbling below the surface and it appeared at the most unexpected times, throwing her off balance. It frustrated her but she was coping. Just.

Turning into a side street, Corinne saw the bar. She was thirsty and decided to take the weight off her feet. Inside it was gloomy, with few customers. A jukebox was churning out trashy songs, songs that reminded her of every bad relationship she'd ever had. At the bar she pulled up a stool and ordered a drink. Before that night with Jack she had never really drunk bourbon. It wasn't to her taste, but a lot had changed since Helena's death and she had come to enjoy the burning sensation it provided.

Jack. She sat there thinking of him as she drank. She had seen him around town many times, but they had danced around each other like two failed lovers, barely uttering two words to each other. She still had no idea who he really was, but she thought about him every day. She had no idea why and it perplexed her greatly, it was as though he was inextricably linked to her in some way, but how she just couldn't figure out.

Shaking thoughts of Jack from her head, her mind wandered back to Jimmy. They had bridged a gap today and she was so pleased. She had missed him and the children so much, and she was happy to have her family back again. She stared deeply into the glass on the surface in front of her, losing herself in thought, as if trying to find and answer to an unfathomable question.

TEN

Jack arrived at the bar. Turning off the engine, he left the car in its usual parking spot before entering the dark and dreary establishment. He was taken aback to see Corinne sitting at the bar. She was the last person he had expected to see. He had caught glimpses of her around town over the last few months, but had done his best to avoid her. He had finally settled, renting a small flat in the town, deciding to face up to his responsibilities once and for all, but that day still hadn't arrived. He was still struggling with his guilt and how he could make amends. Each day he woke with a new plan, he would go to the police, he would sit down, tell them all about the accident, and let the authorities decide what to do with him, but as the hours crept past his bravado failed and he ended up back at square one. Another day gone and he was still a murderer at large. In the end he decided to leave it to the police, let them do their jobs, let them come and find him.

Looking across at Corinne he debated turning round and leaving, but it was his favourite bar, and he wasn't leaving it for fear of having to talk to a woman.

As Corinne drank she felt the presence of someone next to her. She looked up. Jack. It was as though thinking of him minutes earlier had conjured him, and it threw her off balance.

He pulled up a stool and sat next to her, running his fingers through his hair, which was still a messy length.

"You're the last person I expected to see here."

Corinne shrugged and stared back into her glass. After a lengthy pause she finally spoke.

"Have you been here before?"

"It's my local."

"Ah. Is it always this quiet?"

"Yep. It's why I like it."

The silence descended once more, and Jack filled it by indicating his usual to the bartender. Corinne looked at Jack, trying to gauge him, but he was completely expressionless.

She spoke again, desperate to break the tension that always seemed to exist between them.

"We had the inquest today."

Jack felt his heart beat faster. It had been a tense few months, waiting to be questioned or arrested, expecting every knock at the door to be the police. He expected to hear that witnesses had been found, or that he'd been seen, his car recognised, but nothing had come, and he'd been left alone. He couldn't believe how lucky he had been. Not going to the police had been the right thing to do after all. He was a selfish man whose self-preservation came before anything else.

He had considered going to the inquest, but decided to stay away, he hadn't wanted to intrude on a private affair. The longer he left it, the worse things would be for him and, despite the guilt that was eating him up, he had a strong want to protect himself. He had reached a point where it was too late to give himself up now.

"What was the verdict?"

"An accident. They couldn't track the bastard down, let alone convict him."

"Him? How do you know it was a man? It could have been a woman."

Corinne snorted. "Women aren't that

heartless."

Jack laughed nervously, "How do you figure that?"

Corinne turned to stare at him. It was as though her eyes burned right into his soul, and it made him feel uncomfortable. He felt the sweat rise on his palms, his heart raced and his mouth went dry. He slugged back some of the liquid, to help ease the dryness, but the relief was fleeting. He should have learned by now that booze would never help ease the pain or rid the guilt he felt.

He heard Corinne speaking again.

"To run a woman down and not stop, to not even report it to the police. It was heartless, and not a thing a woman would do. It had to be a man. I just don't understand what goes through someone's head when they do something like that. It was a senseless act and whoever did it should be punished."

Jack knew she was right. It *was* a senseless and heartless act, and he was the one who had made her and her family suffer. He should have owned up, he should have had the guts to be a real man and admit his guilt whatever the consequences, but it was much too late for that. It had become too complicated. He dreamed of them every night: Helena's dead, battered and bruised body merging with Corinne's sweet beautiful, grief stricken face, a face that he wanted to kiss greedily, a body that he wanted to satisfy. Was he falling in love with her or was it just his pathetic, screwed up mind, trying to find a way of assuaging the guilt? He was utterly ashamed of himself and yet here he was still talking to her, pretending to be a friend, still turning up in her life. What the hell was wrong with him?

"Don't upset yourself Corinne. Let me get you another drink."

Placing a hand on her bare arm, he leaned in to the bartender to order another drink.

Waves of dizziness crashed over Corinne in an instant and everything became dark and fuzzy. The bar in front of her merged with the blurred interior of a car and she found herself sitting in the driver's seat. It was night and pitch black, her hands were on the steering wheel but she had no control over the vehicle. It was moving at full speed along a dark road. She tried to work out where she was but the answer eluded her. To her left, a frightened animal scuttled away from the car, disappearing quickly from view. A church appeared to her right and suddenly from nowhere there she was.

Helena. Standing in the road ahead of her.

Her sister turned too late, too late to see the car that was already upon her. Corinne stared in horror as the sickening crunch of the car hitting the fragile body filled the car. Helena was thrown high into the air and Corinne screamed and blacked out.

"Corinne! Come on Corinne, wake up!" A panicked voice punctured the air around her, pulling her through the blackness and back to the surface.

Slowly, as she came to, Corinne found herself back in the bar. The room had stopped swaying, the dizziness was subsiding and the darkness had decreased. Jack was beside her, arm around her shoulder trying his best to help her up from the floor.

"Jack?"

"You took one hell of a tumble there. Maybe you should see a doctor."

She looked at him for a moment, before shaking him loose and grabbing her bag. She was confused. She hadn't had a vision in months and suddenly Jack turns up and they start again. Why did that always happen when he was around? She certainly knew how to make a bloody fool of herself. She needed to get away, she needed to think. This vision had been more prominent than the others. It had meant something. She needed the cards; they would tell her.

"I'm sorry Jack but I have to go."

She ran from the bar as fast as her wobbly legs could carry her, leaving Jack staring into his glass with confusion. He was quiet with his thoughts for a few minutes, before asking for another drink. Digging into his jacket pocket he found the silver locket and flipped it open. He had gotten a good look at Corinne's locket as she tumbled off the stool and it was identical to the one in his hand. Opening the trinket, he looked at the photo of Corinne staring back at him. He knew every part of her face, the colour of her eyes, the way her hair fell over her shoulders. He had studied it for so long he felt he knew everything there was to know, except for her touch and that was the one thing he desperately wanted but couldn't have. Closing the locket, he placed it safely back in his jacket pocket before downing his drink and leaving the confines of the bar.

ELEVEN

Corinne finally made it home. She had needed the fresh air but the walk took longer than expected and she was exhausted. It had been a long, emotional day and she was feeling worn out with it all. Just as she placed a key in the lock, a shadowy figure appeared by her side.

"Shit! Jesus Jack, you scared the hell out of me. What are you doing here?"

"I don't think you should be alone tonight."

"And why's that?"

"Because you're upset."

"I'm absolutely fine."

As she turned to enter her house, Jack tried following but she stopped him, firmly placing her hand on his chest. The room span and tilted, dizziness overwhelmed her once more and she was incapable of stopping the enveloping darkness that overwhelmed her.

The moon was high, shining brightly. Corinne found herself standing in the middle of the road. Everything around her was hazy, but as she turned she could clearly see Helena lying on the tarmac at her feet. Blood seeped through her sister's clothing, pooling on the tarmac at her side, her eyes wide and slowly glazing over. Life ebbing away as the seconds passed. Corinne knew even before she knelt to her aid, that there was nothing she could do for her.

Her sister was dead.

Bones were shattered.

Neck was broken.

A life taken.

A noise behind her made her turn, and she caught sight of a car disappearing into the distance. She squinted trying to read the number plate but all she could make out was the blaze of rear lights in the darkness. Turning back to her sister she ran a hand over her beautiful golden hair, her fingers tingling at the touch, as the last essence of her sister's life passed through her before it was lost forever. In that brief moment Corinne felt whole again, and the grief waned slightly, but all too soon the moment had passed and the heaviness of loss descended again and she knew Helena was gone forever.

Everything turned hazy and as she cried out her sister's name, Corinne found herself back in her own hallway. She was on the floor slumped against the wall, supported by Jack, her hand still on his chest.

"Goddamn it!" Corinne exclaimed before pushing him away, hauling herself to her feet and storming into the front room. Jack quietly closed the front door behind him. He removed his jacket, throwing it over the banisters before following her. He stood there leaning on one of the chairs, watching as Corinne lit the mantelpiece candle. Once done, she sat.

"I lost someone once too."

Corinne barely heard him and continued to stare up at the candle. The visions were becoming stronger and she had no idea what was causing them or why they were happening, but with each episode it was as though she were being handed another piece of a puzzle that was slowly revealing what had happened to her sister. What confounded her was why did they happen when Jack was around? Was he somehow connected? Her head pounded from too much thinking.

Jack continued to lean on the chair, watching her, as equal measures of confusion and fatigue continued to pass across her face. It was as though something perplexed her and she was trying to work through a solution in her head. Out of the corner of his eye, he saw a brown leather journal resting on the mantelpiece. He reached forward and lifted it.

Corinne caught the movement and immediately dragged herself back to reality.

"Don't touch that!" she snapped.

Shrugging, he replaced it before finally taking a seat in the chair opposite. He paused a moment before breaking the silence.

"She was only eighteen years old."

Confused, Corinne tilted her head.

"Who was?"

"The person I lost. She was my girlfriend."

Corinne didn't respond. She sat there and stared, so he continued. He needed to tell her, needed to explain. "We were driving home from a party and an oncoming car careered out of control and hit us, we crashed into a tree. Nikki was driving, and they say she died upon impact. The man who hit us had been banned from driving." He paused once more, unsure of how to continue. Looking up he met Corinne's eyes. They had softened and he knew she was giving him the permission he needed to bare his soul.

"Nikki died and I survived. I shouldn't have,

but I did. I wish I could go back and change things. I have re-lived that night so many times. I should have been the one driving. Maybe if I had, I could have controlled the car, maybe we wouldn't have crashed and maybe Nikki would still be alive now. But she isn't. I can't change any of it. It's consigned to history and so I have to carry it with me every day, until I die. It never goes away, ever."

Corinne reached forward to gently take his hand in hers.

"I'm so sorry for what happened Jack, but it wasn't your fault."

"Whether it was my fault or not, it doesn't change how I feel. What I'm trying to say Corinne, is that I know exactly what you're going through."

"I appreciate the sentiment Jack, but how can you? Helena was my *twin*. We had a connection, stronger than anything else. It's like part of me died when she died, like a piece of me is missing and always will be, like I will never be whole again."

"I understand, honestly I do, and I know you loved her. Of course you did; she was your sister. I'm trying to tell you, you're not the only one who has suffered Corinne. I loved Nikki. We were getting married. She was the love of my life, and I feel responsible for what happened. Even though you had nothing to do with your sister's accident, you still feel responsible for what happened, just like I do for Nikki's death. But you will get over it. You can't carry the guilt forever, Corinne."

She stared deeply into those beautiful dark haunting eyes of his, and knew he was right. She broke down, her tears falling fast and furious. The floodgates had opened, and there was little she could do to stop them. Jack had gotten to the crux of the matter; she *did* feel guilty. She had always felt like she was the older sister and needed to protect Helena. Since Helena's death, she felt like she had let her down. She should have done more to look after her, but really, what could she have done? Helena was an adult and if there was one thing Corinne knew about her sister it was that she was her own woman. No one had ever been able to control her or tell her what to do.

Jack knelt before Corinne and pulled her from the chair into his arms, comforting her. He rocked her gently and stroked her hair, enjoying the feel of her in his arms, finally able to be close to her. Corinne clung to him and sobbed like a child, releasing all the pent up grief and emotion that had simmered beneath the surface since that fateful day.

They stayed there on the floor in the light of the crackling fire, until finally her tears ceased and she looked up at him, smiling weakly. Before she could speak, Jack gently brushed his lips against hers, testing the waters. Corinne, desperate for love, greedily accepted, needing and wanting his comfort in whatever form it came. She wanted it never to end. It was a way to block out all of the hurt and pain, and she succumbed to him wholeheartedly. She ran her fingers through his unkempt hair as he slid them both to the floor, and they lay there, slowly removing each other's clothing, exploring each other's bodies, making love in the fire lit gloom until both were satisfied and spent. As the night finally darkened, the moon cast its eerie glow through the window, enhancing the curves of their bodies as they lay dozing in each other's arms in the warmth of the fire's dying embers.

TWELVE

Corinne awoke with a start, feeling disoriented. It took her a moment to realise she was naked in her own bed. The covers had been placed across her midriff, and her hair was loose and flowed across the pillow in shimmering golden waves. She smiled remembering the previous evening. It had been a long time since she had given herself so freely to a man, and she bathed in the warm glow she felt. Reaching out, she felt for Jack but he wasn't there; only a vague warmth and faint indentation in the sheets remained to show he'd ever been there.

Climbing from the comfortable warmth, she pulled on her robe and padded downstairs to the front room in search of him. The fire had been damped down and the candles extinguished. As she looked at herself in the mirror, she spied the table behind her in the reflection.

Her tarot box was open and the cards had been spread across the table. One single card lay face up on top of the others, and her heart thudded nervously, as she stepped closer.

The Lovers.

Next to the box were two lockets, one with a chain and one without. Reaching for her neck, she realised hers had been removed. The other locket was Helena's. Her sister's missing locket. Ice crept into her heart as the final piece of the puzzle fell into place.

Jack had murdered Helena.

*

As Jack drove through the town, a burning cigarette hung from his lips and smoke wafted through the car. He had crept out of Corinne's house in the early hours after putting her to bed, where she fell asleep instantly. The guilt he felt before was nothing to how he felt now; he had completely taken advantage of her, and it was utterly shameful. He knew there was an ill wind blowing and it was now only a matter of time before the situation was removed from his hands and the truth came out. He'd had enough of running, enough of lying, enough of the guilt. It was time to face up to the consequences of his actions, whatever they may be.

*

Corinne sat at the table with a coffee in her trembling hands. After sipping the warm brew, she placed the cup to one side and gathered up the tarot cards. Shuffling them, she placed the upturned *Lovers* card back into the pack. She lifted the lockets and the dizziness hit her immediately forcing her to pass out. She hit the floor with a hollow thud.

Morning had flicked to night and she was standing in the road. It was deathly quiet, the church stood at the roadside, dark and foreboding, bats flying around its belfry. The full moon shone brightly, casting an ethereal glow over everything. Looking around, Corinne tried to find Helena. Maybe all this was meant to be a way of saving her? If she could find her, maybe Corinne could somehow tell her not to cross the road? But Helena was nowhere to be found. Shifting uncomfortably on her feet, Corinne glanced down.

What the hell?

Her feet were bare.

As her eyes scanned upwards, she saw Helena's favourite sandals dangling from her fingers, and she was wearing a dress Helena had bought a few months back when the twins had gone shopping together. On Corinne's shoulder was her missing handbag that she had spent three weeks searching for, before realising Helena had borrowed it without asking. In the moonlight a sparkle caught her eye and she saw she was wearing the wedding band Jimmy had given to Helena on their wedding day.

Now she was completely freaked out.

Had she somehow switched places with her sister? If so, why? She spun around in the road, looking for a sign, some clue that would tell her what was happening. All of a sudden a car turned the corner. The driving was too fast and erratic for the small side street. Corinne watched as the car swerved and narrowly avoided hitting a fox.

In that briefest of moments, realisation hit her. She had seen this before, but from other perspectives. With mounting fear and dread she knew what would come next. The car was heading straight for her, the headlights were bright and dazzled her momentarily, but as it got closer she saw the driver. It was a man and he and he was distracted, he wasn't looking at the road ahead. Then suddenly he lifted his head but it was too late, the brakes screeched as the car skidded out of control. As the car hit her, she stared directly at the driver.

Jack.

Screaming with pain Corinne felt the bones throughout her body shatter. Her internal organs bruised, split and failed and her heart slowed as she hit the ground with a thud. She blacked out, the pain of her broken body too much to bear.

*

Gasping for air, Corinne came round on her living room floor. Once the grogginess had subsided she rolled over, taking in her surroundings.

She was home. She was alive!

It had only been a vision. She was lying next to the table, and she sat up to catch her breath and steady herself. The lockets were still in her hand, and her head was pounding from where she must have hit it on the way down.

She stood and placed the lockets on the mantelpiece either side of the photo of her and her sister before returning to the table. Picking up the tarot deck, she reshuffled it before selecting cards to read. Slowly, one by one, she turned them over and carefully studied them.

The meaning of each one hit home and she finally saw the whole story clearly.

She now knew what she had to do.

*

Jack pulled the car into the space outside the

bar. He had been expecting it to be open as usual but the sign read 'Closed'. Shrugging, he leaned over, opened the glove box and took out a bottle. Getting out of the car, he locked it securely before walking along the road, swigging from the bottle as he went.

He was even fed up of driving. It hadn't been the same since the accident. A thing that used to bring him such joy and comfort now caused him only pain and misery. In fact, his whole life caused him pain and misery. He would walk until he found somewhere else that was open, or maybe he would just do everyone a favour and find the nearest bridge and jump. As he walked, he thought about the previous night. Despite his growing feelings for her, he hadn't intended to sleep with Corinne, it had just happened. It must have been the grief; it did funny things to people. She had been so upset, all he had wanted to was comfort her, and then one thing had led to another. In the cold light of day he had regretted his actions. As if it wasn't enough to kill Helena, he then had to go and sleep with her sister when she was at her lowest.

He shook his head. "Nice touch Jack, well done," he muttered to himself.

As the wind whistled along the street, he looked up at the sky, where dark clouds were brewing overhead. The air had become heavy, laden with the promise of a storm.

Never a good sign.

*

Jack had killed Helena.

Corinne felt sick to the stomach. Jack had befriended her, acted like he had cared, then lied to her, slept with her, even had her feeling sorry for him, and all the while he was playing her. She was disgusted with herself for being stupid enough to fall for it.

What made a person do that? How could he be so twisted and evil?

He had even gone on about his precious girlfriend who had died in a car accident. Was that all just an elaborate lie too? She paced the room, the anger building and swelling within her. She was furious, he had hurt her deeply, a very bad combination. She was trying to think of what she should do. Maybe she should call the police, tell them all about it, they would go and arrest him and justice would be done. She stopped pacing and stared at the photo of her and Helena, shaking her head. What would she say to the police? She didn't know where Jack lived and didn't even know his last name. The police would never believe her. What proof did she actually have?

Absolutely none.

All she had was a locket that could have been found and returned to her by a sympathetic bystander, a tarot reading and some visions.

They would laugh her out of town.

There was only one thing she could do, and she knew exactly where Jack would be. Corinne extinguished the candles, before pulling on her coat and grabbing her bag. Moments later she was crossing town in a taxi to collect her car from Jimmy's house.

*

Jack was still walking the streets. The alcohol was sliding down far too easily and with each step he was becoming more confused and unstable on his feet. Turning the corner he saw the church ahead and the spot where the accident happened. How the hell did that happen? Why did life always bring him back to this?

Shrugging to himself, he carried on walking. He didn't care what happened now. He would turn himself in and be done with it all; let someone else decide his fate for him. He had almost reached the church and was swaying dramatically, barely able to stand. Clouds now massed overhead and the air smelt heavily of rain. His vision was blurred from the effects of the alcohol that was burning through his body, and he stood at the edge of the road watching the impending storm.

*

Corinne collected her car and drove to the bar. Rattling the doors she realised it was closed. She could see Jack's car parked across the road, but he was nowhere to be found. She was at a loss as to what to do. This was the only place she knew where to find him. She got back in her car and set off towards her house, her mind turning over and over. She needed to find him, she needed to talk to him, to ask him why. Why had he done it? Why had he just driven away without telling anyone? Why had he taken advantage of her?

Dark clouds that suited her mood rolled in, and large droplets of rain began to fall. The air was hot and heavy and buzzed with the approaching electrical storm. Flicking a switch she concentrated on the road as her wipers moved quickly, dispersing the fast falling water. She decided to take a shortcut so she could get home and out of the wretched weather. As she turned the corner she realised her drive had taken her to the street where Helena had died.

How had she ended up here? This wasn't the right direction. How many times was she to make this journey in her lifetime? It was as though fate had hold of her and was guiding her, and she was just a passenger along for the ride.

*

Jack had taken his last slug of booze, he shook the bottle but it was definitely empty. He grinned to himself. Maybe his good friend, alcohol, would finally kill him? He could always live in hope.

It was now pouring with rain and the water seeped into his clothes and drenched his hair, slicking it to his head. Tipping the bottle back once more, he tried to suck the remaining dregs from the bottom. He gave up; it had nothing left to give. Frustrated, he flung the bottle at the wall and it shattered, spewing sharp splinters of glass across the pavement. Stepping back into the road, he stared at the church, before spinning round, stumbling, stepping blindly. Street lights blurred and everything appeared before him in doubles.

He wanted it over with. He didn't deserve to live. All he wanted was Nikki, but she was gone to him forever. He wanted peace, was it too much to ask?

"Come on! I don't deserve my life!" he yelled in an alcohol-fuelled tirade. "Just take me!"

The clouds were darker now and lightning

flashed across the sky, casting eerie shadows. A large ground-shaking rumble of thunder quickly followed it. The rain was torrential now, soaking everything in its reach. Jack felt the rain on his skin, and the sizzle of electricity as lightning struck again, landing across the street.

"Is that all you've got?" he screamed to the heavens. "Pitiful! Come on, do your worst. I'm ready for it! Give me all you got!"

He stood in the road, screaming at the heavens like a madman, taunting the storm as it raged on around him.

*

As the lightning flashed, Corinne saw him ahead of her, yelling and stumbling in the road, angry at the whole world, and she knew that their future had already been written. She didn't need tarot or visions this time. Fate was being decided before her very eyes. She knew that what was about to happen was always meant to be. Driving towards him, she pressed the accelerator hard; the needle on the dashboard climbed steadily as her hands tightly gripped the steering wheel. Not once did her eyes waver from the road ahead. Not once did she falter in her decision.

As Jack turned, it was already too late.

The crunch was sickening, his bones

fractured and he was thrown high into the air. Corinne braked hard. Tyres squealed noisily as the car slid along the slickly wet tarmac and brakes emitted acrid smoke into the air. Jack's body bounced on the roof of the car before finally landing on the asphalt with a thud of broken skin and bone.

Jumping from the car, Corinne ran back to him. Large drops of rain pelted her, the wind whipped at her clothes, and thunder cracked loudly overhead, shaking everything, as dark menacing clouds were punctured by forks of bright hot lightning.

Standing over Jack's body she watched as he took his last few breaths. Blood flowed from his lifeless corpse, staining the tarmac, and his eyes flickered in a last brief fight for life. She could barely breathe, and her heart beat fast and hard within her chest.

Jack was dead.

"That was for Helena," she whispered hoarsely, before running back to her car and speeding away.

*

Corinne stood at the window and watched as the rain finally ceased, and the clouds slowly parted, allowing a weak sun to brighten the world. The wind had dropped to a light breeze, the thunder was now barely a whisper in the distance, and the lightning a mere flicker on the horizon. All of the guilt, hurt and despair had disappeared, and relief had begun to flood through her body. Her life was once more her own and she would live it to the fullest, not just for her but also for her sister.

"I love you Helena," she whispered as she extinguished the memorial candle for the last time, the pain and loss of her sister's death finally behind her.

Acknowledgements

Thank you to Chris Joyce for the amazing book cover design, Dale Cassidy and Laura Barclay for editing and proof reading and Clare Ayala for the fantastic formatting.

To my supportive friends, especially Dee Thompson, Ailsa Burns and Alyson Fennell, you constantly support me by listening to my ideas and reading though my manuscripts. You're the best guys! A special thanks to everyone at WLC, especially Melissa Foster, Sass Cadeaux, Rayne Cullen and Kathie Shoop. I have learned so much from you!

To my family, who have been there for me constantly over the years and put up with my chaotic life, I love you all very much. To my husband T, Integrate wouldn't have been possible without you, thank you for being my partner in crime.

Finally, thank you to everyone who has read Integrate. You took a chance on me and bought the book and for that I am very grateful.

About the Author

Chrissie Parker lives in London UK, with her husband.

Twitter - @chrissie_author

Facebook -
https://www.facebook.com/ChrissieParkerAuthor

Web – www.chrissieparker.com

5874617R00066

Printed in Great Britain
by Amazon.co.uk, Ltd.,
Marston Gate.